M. B. M. Tolan

Eudora, a Tale of Love

M. B. M. Tolan

Eudora, a Tale of Love

ISBN/EAN: 9783743388505

Manufactured in Europe, USA, Canada, Australia, Japa

Cover: Foto ©Andreas Hilbeck / pixelio.de

Manufactured and distributed by brebook publishing software
(www.brebook.com)

M. B. M. Tolan

Eudora, a Tale of Love

A TALE OF LOVE

BY

M. B. M. TOLAND.

AUTHOR OF

ÆGLE AND THE ELF,
THE INCA PRINCESS,
IRIS,
SIR RAE. ETC., ETC.

Eudora's love, with varied light and shade,
By Ella from fond memories portrayed.

WITH DRAWINGS BY
H. SIDDONS MOWBRAY AND W. H. GIBSON.

AND DECORATIONS IN THE TEXT BY   L. S. IPSEN.

PHILADELPHIA:
J. B. LIPPINCOTT COMPANY.
LONDON: 10 HENRIETTA ST. COVENT GARDEN.
1888.

FIGURE DRAWINGS BY H. SIDDONS MOWBRAY.

DRAWINGS

LANDSCAPES DRAWN BY W. HAMILTON GIBSON.

CANTO I.

How changed is everything!

EUDORA

I.

At home once more;

     And yet it does not seem
Those twice ten years were other than a dream,
Instead of absent life in distant land.
How changed is everything!

     The sparkling sand
That bedded my pet brook is overgrown
With marshy reeds, as though it ne'er had known
The rushing waterfall that bounded o'er
Its pebbled barrier in days of yore.
Bright, laughing wavelets leapt the livelong day,
Kissing the willows with foam-flecks of spray,
Dancing between the flowery borders steep
Into a cove of placid waters deep.

11

I gaze bewildered at the stately trees,
Erewhile but bushes swayed by slightest breeze,
When last I saw them with my childhood's friend,
Whose strange romance with memories fond I blend.

II.

Eudora perfect beauties all combined
Of noble presence, lovely and refined;
Her smiles indenting dimples on her face,
Fair as the *Nymphœa Alba*,—with rare grace
Of Grecian features, and large dreamy eyes,
The azure deepening like the evening skies;
Their heavenly depths an undecided hue,
Beaming with glances ever pure and true.
Her golden hair, when left to fall unbound
In sunny waves trailed coiling on the ground;
Unconscious of her artless, winning way,
She lent indulgence to my love of play,
The haunting mirthful fun forever near
That oft provoked some sportive prank to cheer.

III.

One morn we stood beside the sparkling rill,
And watched the fall with foaming waters fill;
The bubbling pool in murmured measures gay
Awaking ever some sweet roundelay:
Eudora sang the while enchantingly
That charming song of purest melody—
The sweetest madrigal the Laureate wrote,
His speaking "Brook"—each rippling liquid note
Breathes harmony through all the rhythmic lines
Which music in true poesy enshrines.
To the clear warbled measures as she sang,
The lilies nodded, and the echoes rang
With fairy voices floating on the air
Of unseen choristers from everywhere.

IV.

The song had scarcely ceased, when through the brush
Rang out a shot.   Down fell a wounded thrush
Before Eudora's feet, and flutt'ring died.
Then followed footsteps;—quickly to her side,

Breaking the boughs, a youthful hunter came;
Lifting his hat, he smiled, and took the game
Eudora offered with a trembling hand.
His admiration he could not command,
At sight of such enchanting charms amazed,
Beaming with wonder and delight he gazed.
His lingering glance, as slowly he withdrew,
Kindled her blushes to my furtive view;
Inspired my muse in merry jest to write
Impromptu lines,—suggestive numbers light:—

IMPROMPTU

Thy song the sportsman surely heard,
   For thou didst sing so sweetly;
Enraged, he shot the rival bird
   That drowned thy voice completely.

Lo, when he came to seek his game,
   Meantime the songstress seeking,
His glance betrayed his heart aflame,
   With admiration speaking.

14

Thy blushes and thy downcast eyes
    At once thy thoughts betraying,
Thy timid glance of pleased surprise,
    Thy heart its throbs delaying.

He bears the haughty hermit's name,
    Poetical and pretty ;
Last evening to the Bluff he came,
    This subject of my ditty.

V.

Eudora, laughing, read the lines and said,
" Why are you, Eila, by wild fancies led ?
Why write such nonsense ?
                    Why forever tease ?
Your pleasant raillery may fail to please.
Often I wonder why my dearest friend
Her happy thoughts with mimicry will blend."
" You wonder still," I answered.   " Fie ! oh, fie !
The arrows from my bow fall harmlessly ;
I aim my pointless shafts at those I love,
And thus my fondness for my friends I prove."

15

Then twining arms we slowly sauntered home.
When near the Bluff, I pointed to the dome
Or cupola that crowned its tower of stone
Where dwelt a hermit until now alone.
A stranger,—Alvin Alster,—nothing more
Was known of him; to all he closed his door.
Secluded from the busy stage of life
He mixed not with the world; no care, no strife
Disturbed him in his search of mystic lore
From valued tomes that formed his hoarded store.

VI.

A house half hidden by the wild woodbine,
And ivy mingling with sweet eglantine,
That climbed the latticed casement, draping o'er
The Gothic pillars of the oaken door;
Trailing along the tufted moss-grown sod,
Save by the hermit's footsteps seldom trod.
Here all alone he passed the cheerless day,
Till unexpected came his kinsman gay,—

A youth of nineteen years, perhaps,—not more,—
Of the same name the Solitary bore;
Accustomed at his military school
To discipline severe, of strictest rule,
He heeded not the hermit's cold reserve,
Hoping in time his better mood to serve;
And with a heart from selfish motives free,
For his strange host he felt deep sympathy.
Last of his name upon his father's side,
He came to seek his kinsman lone, whose pride
Had closed his heart to every tie of blood,
Until this namesake on his threshold stood.

VII.

That evening when the dying twilight pale
O'er the still landscape spread her dewy veil,
The violets, all nestled in their bed,
Through webs of gossamer sweet fragrance shed;
The morning-glories their fair faces closed,
With drooping heads in silent sleep reposed;

For Nature, gentle mother, on her breast
Had lulled her floral progeny to rest.
Eudora sought her home not far from ours,
A cottage clad with many climbing flowers,
Closing her visit with the closing day.
Fondly I watched her wend the sylvan way,
Until she entered her embowered door,
And the young sportsman stood our gate before,
With pleasant greeting and true genial grace
Within our group he found a welcome place.
My parents soon a lively interest took
In our adventure by the babbling brook,
Which he related in becoming style:
As if suppressing secret mirth, the while
He glanced expectantly with his dark eyes—
"I come," he added, "to apologize."
My father laughing, said, "That wild resort
Is tempting to such incidents of sport."
Then asked of me, "Is not Eudora here?"
And when I answered, he, with social cheer,
Said, merrily, "Eudora well could spare

18

Fondly I watched her wend the sylvan way

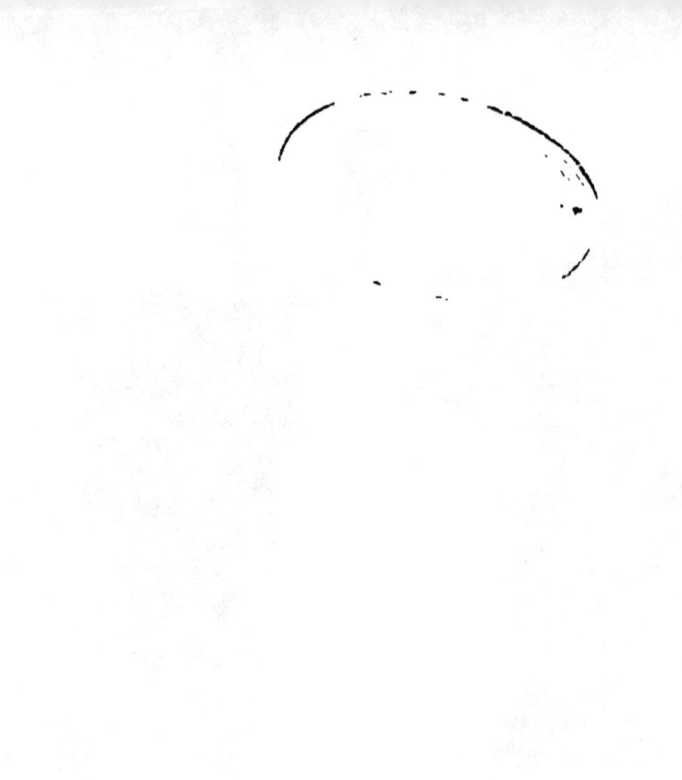

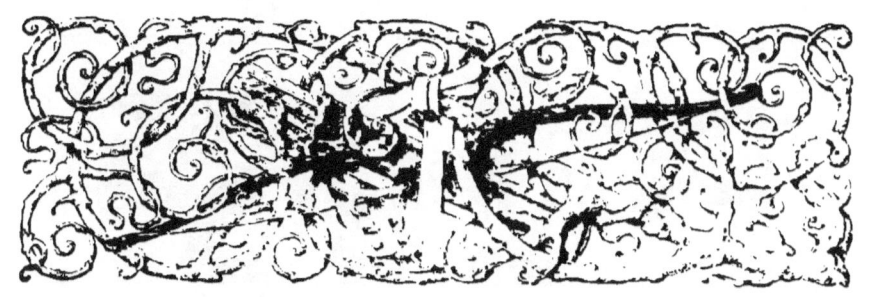

From her rich golden treasures, tresses fair,
Enough to make Puck's girdle round the world,
Of silken sheen, in radiant sunbeams furled."
The generous compliment was well repaid
By the delight our visitor displayed.
My mother, pleased to join our pleasantry,
Added, "Such charms as hers we seldom see.
All must admire with rapture and surprise
The perfect beauty; but sad thoughts will rise,
Predicting what may be her future fate?"
My father interrupted, " Do not prate
Thus dolefully of one with heart so pure,
Her future happiness we may insure."
I caught his hand in mine exclaiming, " True,
The brightest destiny to her is due."
Smiling, our guest took leave. " Good-night," said he;
" My host demands an early hour of me."

VIII.

" A fine companion for the Solitaire,"
My father said. " Can he be happy there?"

My mother made reply, " That happy face
Presages joy and peace in any place.
A young Cadet, so chivalrous, will cheer
The stern old Sage, his kinsman ;—yet I fear
That stolid hermit never will consent
To social pastimes with his neighbors spent.
So long accustomed to his lonely life,
He shuns the world as if 'twere naught but strife."
Much more we pondered on the strange recluse,
Till midnight brought to our discourse a truce.
With parting kiss and blessing I retired,
In pensive mood by happy hopes inspired.

IX.

Sleeping, I dreamed, and in my vision came
Eudora with the stranger,—a bright flame
Like ignis-fatuus gleamed above their brows,
Misleading witness of their plighted vows.
Their faces beamed with perfect happiness,
While near them stood a priest as if to bless

20

The marriage rites God's holy laws command
And join the lovers with the nuptial band;
When came the hermit angrily, and told
The priest his ceremony to withhold.
"These nuptials I forbid! You do not dare,"
He cried, "unite in wedlock such a pair
Of children! He is nothing but a boy
Who yields to his first fancy for a toy."
At his command the holy man withdrew;
The hermit followed with a cold adieu.
Kaleidoscopic scenes then filled the room;
Brilliant reflections, brightening the gloom,
Of wondrous beauties, dazzling with delight,
Until the dawn dispelled the witching sight,
Then from my thoughts forebodings sped away,
And dreams dissolved before the light of day.

X.

The glorious sun was sipping drops of dew
From threads of airy mist, still floating through

21

The tall grass ready to be mown for hay,
Rich with its ruby globes of clover gay,
Tempting the bees to gather honey sweet,
Buzzing from cup to cup until replete
With nectar sipped from countless blossoms fair
That nodded o'er the fields luxuriant there.
The birds were singing to their fledgelings young,
Attempting their first flight the shrubs among;
And anxious mothers wailed with wild unrest
As those they loved forsook the parent nest.

XI.

Beside the brook we often Alvin met,
Where Love his arrows had already whet;
And with unerring aim from supple bow
Had left his mark in blushes warm aglow.
Fate from her distaff spinning fragile thread,
Awaking thoughts by wooing fancies led,
Through warp and woof her graceful shuttle ran,
As she the weaving of the web began.

22

The birds were singing to their fledgelings young.

Page 22.

Thenceforth young Alvin came a frequent guest,
His heart's fond aspirations unrepressed.
Too young as yet to dare avow his choice;
Nor could Eudora find for love a voice,
Save by the glances of her speaking eyes,
Proclaiming her devotion, though unwise;
The coy reserve,—the gentle maiden grace,
The rosy blush that flitted o'er her face,
The struggling hopes, half uttered, half concealed,
And tender gaze her dawning love revealed.
As a third person, it was mine to share
The scenes of loveliness and beauties rare,
While sped the summer on its hasty wing,
Till o'er the landscape, Autumn came to fling
Warm glowing colors with a generous hand,
And scatter gold throughout the smiling land.

CANTO II.

I.

One morn, while pondering o'er some pleasant scheme,
We sauntered slowly by the plashing stream
Until we reached our rest,—a mossy stone;
Where, for a while, Eudora sat alone,
And warbled o'er sweet scraps of melody,
Like liquid voices from the distant sea.
Meanwhile I sought the brightest jewels rare
From Autumn's casket gleaming everywhere;
The gems that decked the maple's ruby crown,
The golden beech and birch of russet brown;
And mingled fern with graceful columbine,
For her fair brow a chaplet to entwine.
The spirit of my mischief—ever near—
Suggested raillery: I would appear
Like victor at the queen of beauty's feet;
And when my frost-gemmed garland was complete,

The offering I laid before her throne
With mimic grace that Alvin would have shown
Eudora, his divinity.   Delight
Beamed on her face with glowing blushes bright,
The while I quoted Leigh Hunt's Letter flowers,
Breathing true love from nature's sunny bowers.

> " An exquisite invention this,
> Worthy of love's most honeyed kiss,
> This art of writing billet-doux
> In buds and odors and bright hues."

II.

" Bright hues, indeed," she said.   " How grandly gay
Is nature's robe this sparkling frosty day ;"
Then paused to listen with expectancy
To every rustling leaf of bush or tree,
Weaving fair visions such as maidens frame,
Blending with future bliss her lover's name.
Soon there responded to her listening ear
The sound of shambling footsteps drawing near,

The sound of shambling footsteps.

As through a briery path the hermit came,
And, with a trembling voice, pronounced her name,
Fixing his eyes with cold and frowning stare
On her fair face, as if its truth to dare,
Exclaiming, "Thou art here, and so I take
This freedom for my youthful cousin's sake.
Ensnared, led captive, by thy witching wiles,
He raves, he dotes upon thy charms and smiles.
The dreaming, foolish boy hopes time will prove
His right to claim thee, queen of heart and love,
Which I forbid!"

      He paused, still scowling there
With lowering glance at wondrous beauty rare;
Her modest blushes blanched before the rage
Of Alvin's kinsman,—evil boding sage;
For he had come to dash her cup of bliss
In broken fragments to the dark abyss
Of hopeless love.

      "Thou speakest not!" he cried;
"Nor have thy looks his words of praise denied;
Not yet at liberty to yield his heart,

From thy alluring charms he must depart."
Crushed by the edict of stern destiny,
Eudora sat in silent misery;
Pale as the lily and with lips compressed,
Her fluttering heart so throbbed within her breast
My anger rose; and standing by her side
In her defence, I to the hermit cried,—
" O, cruel, cruel man !   How dare you speak
Thus to Eudora?

         Why such tortures wreak
Upon young Alvin's friend?

               A heart so true
Deserves all gentleness, not blame from you;
You wrong her, sir, for you have naught to fear;
Naught has been spoken that you might not hear.
Eudora, come!   This is no place for you;
Listen no longer.   Sir! we bid adieu!"
" Ah! then this is the friend—the little Sprite—
Whom Alvin calls ' the beauty's satellite.'
And art thou sure they were not making love?
A worthy friend in need thou'lt surely prove."

His words were spoken with such irony
That from his presence gladly did I flee,
Drawing Eudora from his blighting gaze
'Neath heavy scowling brows o'er eyes ablaze.

III.

And yet, his manner, when we left, was bland
With courtesy,—'twas hard to understand.
He slowly drew the cap from off his head,
And bowed uncovered as we homeward sped.
Eudora, with a strange bewilderment,
In unresisting, hopeless sorrow went
Along the homeward path; the while I tried
To cheer, to comfort, and arouse her pride.
"Eudora, be yourself! he should not see
He has the power to cause such misery."
She answered not; nor did my words appear
Other than idle efforts; naught could cheer
One of those timid natures,—sensitive,—
Who suffer uncomplaining and yet live.

How changed was she,—how cold! Her speaking eyes
Looked dumb with hidden sorrow and surprise.
She would not enter as we reached our door;
Returned no kiss, and pressed my hand no more;
Grown languid, cold, the image of despair,
Without one answering glance she left me there.

IV.

Confused by all that I had heard and seen,
I felt quite powerless my friend to wean
From fancies fond that filled her heart with light,
And shield its budding flower from early blight.
My father, marking my confusion, asked,
"What ails you, child? Pray, what has overtasked
Your patience? Why this disappointed air?
What fancy crossed, or what imagined care?"
Before my answer I could calmly frame
Alvin in haughty indignation came.
My father listened with contracted brows
As Alvin plead his love and plighted vows,

32

"To you, dear sir, her guardian, I must speak
Before a parting interview I seek
With dear Eudora,—or her mother see.
The hermit, in his cold audacity,
No doubt forestalls me, for this very day
He strove to drive Eudora's love away.
A few brief years, and I shall come to claim
My heart's first love to share my joys, my name ;—
So interwoven with my web of life,
She yet shall wear the sacred title,—wife."

v.

Then, as I watched my father's anxious face,
I saw a brightening smile his frown replace,
And, taking Alvin's hand between his own,
He said, "Brave boy! you all my doubts dethrone.
Regard me as your friend : henceforth you share
A place with my young ward : for her my care
Redoubles from this time.
                          Your every word
Came from a noble heart, and, as I heard,

Convinced me how ungenerous were fears
Distrusting dawning manhood's early years.
To you, with truth and honor, so refined
In choice of purity and noble mind,
I trust with confidence.   We may depend
On future years to bring a happy end.
Yes! yes! you need not promise any more."
When Alvin would again his new vows pour
Joy lit his countenance: with faltering voice
He cried, "Dear sir! it makes my heart rejoice
That you will still regard me as your friend,
And my Eudora from all harm defend:
Good-by! no words can half my thanks express."
Taking my hand he said,

                    "May Heaven bless
You, Eila, for your kind and friendly zeal
That nearly warmed the hermit's heart of steel."

VI.

Then came my tears, nor could I longer stay,
But, rushing from his presence, hid away

Within the sanctum of my room, and there
Knelt down in silent, earnest, tearful prayer.
When I arose, I thought of my sweet friend,—
How could I comfort her? What could I send?
Hoping my effort would not prove in vain,
I wrote some lines to soothe Eudora's pain,
With sympathy so deep, naught could express
The struggling hopes that came my love to bless.
Ill could my mind its wandering thoughts engage,
Though fast my pen flew o'er the blotted page
Until completed, when I laid away
The lines for use at some near future day.

VII.

In consultation late we sat that night:
News from our friends filled us with sad affright.
The mother, still unsparing in her blame,
Sternly forbade the mention of his name,
Whose fancy for her daughter plainly told
Our indiscretion,—we had been too bold,—

It was improper, meeting him alone
In woodland bowers.

        The world would not condone
Such folly, nor would gossip's evil tongue
Cease from its knell that ne'er before had rung
Eudora's name.   She should secluded be
Till time from futile fancy set her free.
When Alvin called his sad adieux to pay,
The servant said, " The ladies wish to-day
To be excused."   " I come to bid good-by!"
Cried Alvin;—" they will surely not deny
One moment.   Take my message in, I'll pay
You well!"   The servant said, " I must obey
My orders, sir; nor can I take your gold;
My duty is to do as I am told."

VIII.

Such was the story brought by my old nurse,
Rebecca, who I'm sure made matters worse.
A crotchety old maid, with jealous care

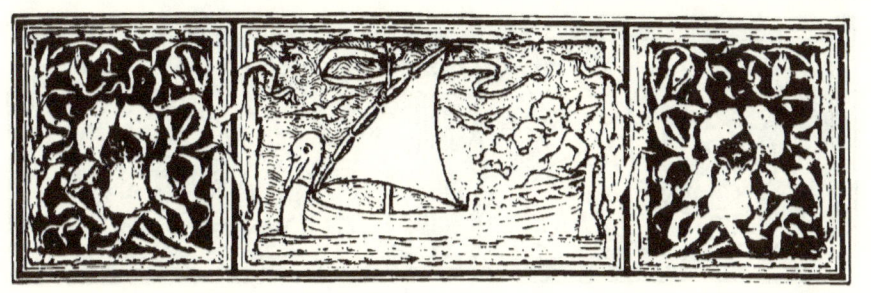

Of one she raised from infancy, nor dare
I doubt her words of gossip nor appear
Even to harbor in my heart a fear
Of her injustice: nor could I believe
Eudora's mother would not soon relieve
Her daughter from all doubts and cruel blame.
'Twas then to interrupt my rev'rie came
Rebecca, prating over errors still;
She censured the stern mother's stubborn will,
Saying, "That woman's tongue goes like a whir,
Nor does she spare you one malicious slur;
She calls you meddlesome, a go-between,
And tries her daughter's heart from you to wean."
Indignantly I cried, "Oh, hush!—Forbear
Repeating evil gossip, and beware
The harm your idle words to us may bring:
From careless gossip slanderous tales oft spring."
"Oh, my! What do I hear?" she sobbing said,
Her apron to her eyes, shaking her head,
"This is the thanks I get,—your nurse, your friend,—
Yet will I ever your good name defend."

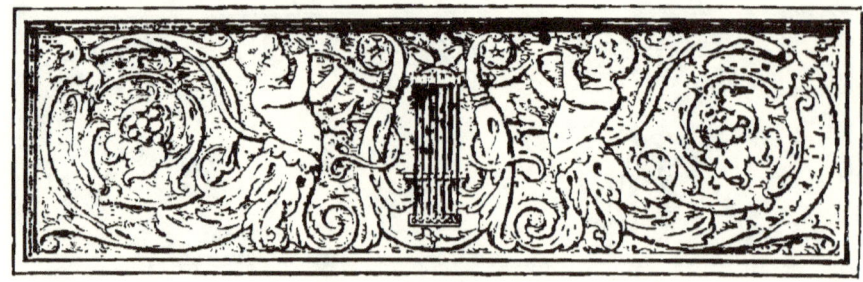

IX.

She hurried from my presence angrily,
Leaving my thoughts in deep perplexity.
My ears were tingling with a sense of shame.
I felt bewildered by the unjust blame,
And pondered thus,—the gossip may be right;
Henceforth let all romances take their flight.
I will be strong enough to do my part
In useful life.   Nonsense from out my heart
Be banished, from this time for evermore.
Donning my shawl, with fear I went before
Eudora's mother, sitting sternly there.
I knelt beside her, clinging in despair
To the one hope that I was still beloved,
And my unselfish motive could be proved.
She pushed me from her so impatiently,
I plead with her, and cried distractedly,
"For dear Eudora's sake! I come to you
With love for her, and my devotion true;
And, as a friend, I wished to let you know
What I feel sure will lighten present woe.

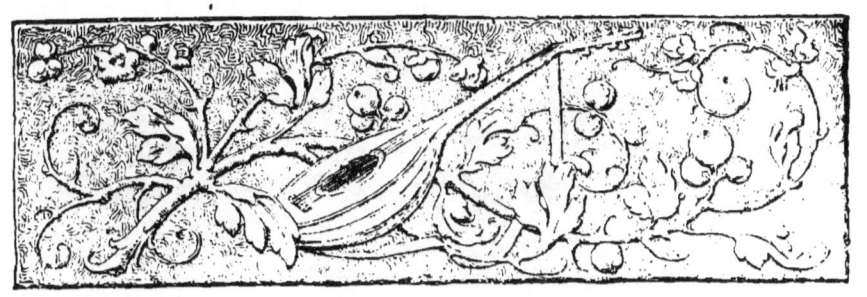

Alvin has sworn to father, he will claim
Eudora soon, to share his love and name."

X.

A softened light her saddened face o'erspread;
She clasped me in her arms and, sobbing, said,
"Pray do not mention that distracted boy!
Eudora's life is blighted.   Her first joy,
By fancy brought, is darkly clouded now.
No word of his—no gallant, manly vow—
Can take the sting from the old hermit's rage,
Who blotted her young life's most blissful page."
Ere she had finished came Eudora, pale,
Submissive, silent; and my words would fail
Half to express the sadness of my heart
Wounded by friendship's sympathetic dart.
I pressed upon her lips my kisses warm,
And strove to drive away the gathered storm.
Feeling that love would other aid demand,
I slipped my crumpled lines within her hand.

39

The watchful mother saw, and sternly said,
"That paper give to me! I've been misled
In trusting such a go-between as you!"
She seized the lines in haste and read them through.

TO EUDORA

Trust in our Lord divine;
Who made the sun to shine
    With radiant light.
Yet 'tis not always day,
Sunbeams dissolve away
    In sombre night.

Then why should mortals weep
If joys they cannot keep
    Within their power?
Sorrow shall pass from thee,
Sweet bliss from trouble free
    Shall charm thy bower.

Night's shadows will have gone
When bright and rosy dawn
   Unveils the sun,
And dries the tears of eve.
So, darling, cease to grieve.
   God's will be done.

XI.

Embracing me again, she checked her tears
And said, " Your words allay a mother's fears.
May Heaven reward you for the spirit shown
That lifts this prayerful tribute to the throne
Of Him who gave us light, the glorious sun ;
And teaches us to say, God's will be done."
Eudora pressed me to her heart awhile,
Blending her kisses with a tearful smile.
And from that hour, amid the gloom, appeared
The dawning sunshine that her young life cheered,
With new-born hope-star shining brilliantly,
Guiding her prayerful thoughts far o'er the sea.

CANTO III.

I.

WINTER, that frigid King, an umpire bold
Between the Sunshine and the North-winds cold,
Sat throned on ice, in robe of purest snow,
His crown of sparkling brilliants bright, aglow
With icicles resplendent, fringing o'er
Incrusted trees that kingly orders wore;
Bedecked was every branch with virgin white,
The roofs and fences shone with crystals bright;
The gloomy clouds soon gathered like a frown
Over the skies, sifting soft snow-flakes down,
Flake chasing flake from the broad canopy,
Drifting o'er fields in swift immensity.
Deep were the drifts obstructing path and road
When ceased the storm. I saw the teamsters goad
Their oxen, ploughing up on either side
The banking snow to make a passage wide.

45

I watched them as they slowly gained the top
Of the high bluff, and then I saw them stop.
The drivers left their teams awhile to rest,
Then ploughed their way and broke through crusted crest
Of one huge bank that blocked the hermitage,
Clearing the path of the secluded Sage.

II.

On their return, after the cut was made,
The teamster signalled to us with his spade;
Rebecca went to learn the mystery.
At her approach he called, excitedly,
"That poor old man up there is nearly dead;
We found him cold and starving in his bed;
Lucky we went there,—he could scarcely speak,
But begged us your young mistress go and seek;
'Tell her,' said he, 'at once to come to me.'"
My mother joined my mission tenderly,
An urgent summons for the doctor sent,
While we to succor the poor hermit went.

Never shall I forget that cheerless scene:
In bed, his heavy coverlets between,
Lay the poor hermit, from a sudden stroke
Of serious illness, struggling as he spoke;
A ghastly smile illumed his shrunken face,
When by his side I sadly took my place.
With feeble voice he faintly whispered me,
"This visit crowns your noblest charity."

III.

A cordial to his lips I held,—he drank,
And vainly strove with faltering voice to thank
In his old stately way.   I shook my head
With finger to my lips.   "Speak not!" I said.
Then as I realized his famished state,
I feared our ministration came too late;
But the good doctor soon relieved my care
By saying, "Partial palsy, and I dare
Express the hope—his constitution strong—
That I may cure him and his life prolong."

47

Then o'er the sufferer's face there passed a flame,
A sudden flush, as if of wakened shame.
"I live," he cried, "a burden. Oh, my God!
Better by far to rest beneath the sod
Than bear such haunting memories as mine,
Without one cheering ray of hope to shine."
Before sleep soothed his agony of mind
He begged the doctor proper aid to find,
Such as he needed until life should end,
Servants and nurse, on whom he could depend.

IV.

The man of skill replied, "Indeed I can,
Husband and wife, a nurse and faithful man:
They shall be here before the close of day."
Turning to me, he added, "You will stay
And minister to him another hour;
Sleep soon will come to soothe with magic power."
Waving his hand toward the patient's bed,
My anxious glance he to the hermit led;

48

The soothing opiate quickly calmed his mind
From harrowing thoughts and memories unkind.
The room was spacious-panelled from the floor;
Around the walls, that antique grandeur wore,
Carvings elaborate, of oak so old
'Twas nearly black, o'erlaid with dusty mould.
Draped with rare tapestries, Diana's chase,
Designed from ancient lore of classic grace.
Here Cynthia and her hounds in full career,
With silver bow pursued the antlered deer.
There stood a cabinet within a niche
With tracery and graven figures rich,
That showed strange work embossed of beauty rare,
Pope, priest, and acolytes depicted there
And time-worn pictures that high art revealed
Through webs the spiders over them had reeled,
All but one face, not beautiful, but fair,
With silver interlacing raven hair,
Like moonbeams shimmering on the night of age.
And in those lineaments, so like the Sage,
The while I studied, I could plainly trace

4

A cruder likeness on the son's pale face.
The library with volumes vellum gray,
All in disorder tumbled, careless lay,
As if untouched for months, each dusty tome,
The mute companions of the hermit's home.
Weaving strange thoughts from wandering fancy's store,
Until the hermit woke, and said, " Before
The doctor comes, let me confess to thee.
Let me my mind from haunting mem'ries free,—
My cruel treatment of the bravest boy
That ever lived, his friends to crown with joy;
For I have dwelt in lonely misery
Since my injustice and cold cruelty.
Thou canst, young lady, make this sorrow less,
If thou wilt write to him what I confess."
My answer pleased him, it was plain to see,
By the soft, tender look he cast on me;
I promised writing, reading, anything
That comfort to his lonely hours would bring.

Then jingling bells we heard; the doctor came,
Followed by two good servants,—man and dame.
Upon the hearth, enframed in antique tile,
Was built a fire of logs, an ample pile,
That sparkling glowed, emitting ruddy rays,
Warming the room with bright and cheerful blaze.
The doctor said, " I'll tell you when to come;
It may be soon."

        At once we hastened home.
My mother sadly said,—

           " The poor old man!
His life must have been wretched, and its span
Has nearly past. Do all you can to please
And comfort him, his troubled mind to ease.
Your letter-writing may make all things well,
But nought of this to dear Eudora tell;
It might distress her; not a single word,
Since Alvin left, of tidings has she heard."
My mother's wish was sacred held by me,
Therefore I kept our secret silently.

VI.

It was not long before the doctor sent
A note that read ;—" The hermit's mind is bent
On the fulfilment of your promise made
To write for him, but I am much afraid
That the excitement may o'ertax his brain.
I write this caution that you may refrain
From subjects irritating, that ensnare
His thoughts; of all such themes you must beware."
When I approached the invalid he smiled,
With greeting that anxiety beguiled,
And said, " I'm thankful thou hast come to ease
My troubled mind, my callous heart to please,
From haunting memories my soul to free :
Thou, like an angel, hast been sent to me.
See ! take this folio, and to Alvin write
All that my heart shall prompt me to indite.

THE LETTER

I.

Dear boy! Forgive my temper rude
  That drove thee from my door:
My blighted heart was not indued
  With hope thy young life bore.

II.

This simple story may explain
  My cold, unsocial mien.
Thy presence caused me poignant pain
  From sorrows I had seen.

III.

When but a child, the luring glance
  Of beauty's witching wiles
Led me into the fatal chance
  That tender youth beguiles.

53

IV.

A maiden fair as sunshine gleams
  The sylvan bowers among,
Threaded a web of blissful dreams,
  Filled with sweet words unsung.

V.

And thou didst blighted hopes recall,
  Sad memories revive,—
When I would fain have banished all
  Nor kept the past alive.

VI.

Ill could I greet with cordial love,
  Or welcome any guest;
Thy grace of youth could not remove
  The sorrows of my breast.

VII.

I loved with strange intensity
  And ardent fond delight,
The idol of my destiny,
  During our childhood's flight.

VIII.

We lived as neighbors all our days,
    And with our growth I loved ;
Playing the hero in our plays
    Too proud when she approved.

IX.

My tutors never tried to wean
    My heart from love's fond flame
I lavished on my bosom's queen,—
    Nor did they chide, nor blame.

X.

Time glided on with dancing tread,
    Nor stayed for love's delays.
The parting filled my soul with dread
    When came my college days.

XI.

How fair she looked.   How brightly glanced
    Her eyes, the hue of night.
Her farewell words my heart entranced
    With sad yet fond delight.

55

XII.

Her raven tresses o'er a brow
　Pure as the Alpine snow;
Her lips—I think I see them now—
　Curved like the Archer's bow.

XIII.

So winsome in her pleasantry,
　'Twas hard to bid adieu;
I kissed her hand with gallantry,
　And sadly I withdrew.

XIV.

No day, no hour, no moment fled
　Unladen with my sighs;
Until my disappointment led
　To hasty step unwise.

XV.

I left my college, hurried home,
　My love once more to see,
Determined ne'er again to roam,
　From studies to be free.

56

XVI.

How stealthily I reached the hall,
   Expecting glad surprise :
And there before me, I recall
   A scene that dazed my eyes.

XVII.

The treasure of my heart, beloved,
   Sat clasped in the embrace
Of a swarth foreigner, who proved
   Usurper of my place.

XVIII.

She left his arms and smiling said,
   " Why Alvin ! art thou here ?
By spirit of some mischief led,
   Thou truant boy, I fear."

XIX.

Then, laughing lightly, as she gazed
   In the dark stranger's face,
Exclaimed, " Marquis ! art thou amazed ?
   Dost thou no likeness trace ?

XX.

" The hero of the tale I told
　　Last eve ?　This is the child,
My infant friend ; but now too old
　　To nurse his fancy wild.

XXI.

" Alvin !　This is my lord to be :
　　And so will be thy friend.
The Marquis de la Platrovi :—
　　Thy childish dream must end."

XXII.

Thus she presented me to him
　　With mimic courtesy.
My blood ran cold, and sight grew dim,
　　Dazed by her raillery.

XXIII.

And from that moment I desired
　　To leave a world of strife,
And live in solitude retired
　　The studious hermit's life.

58

Thenceforth, a dull recluse alone,
　　A dreary life I led.
My blood was chilled, my heart like stone,
　　To love's fond impulse dead.

Years rolled on years, until there came
　　A message; the last breath
My father drew, he called my name
　　Before his sudden death.

My mother wrote, "Alvin! Dear son,
　　Haste to our saddened home!
Thou art my child, the only one
　　To comfort me. Pray come!"

I answered, " Never home again!
　　Dear mother."—That fond word
Thrilled through my heart with waking pain
　　And whispered I had erred.

XXVIII.

Wrapped in my selfish solitude,
    And armed with cynic pride,
I felt my spirit quite subdued
    By thoughts that still would chide.

XXIX.

Then passed a few short years—no more—
    When documents were sent
That my dear mother's blessing bore
    With her last testament.

XXX.

My ample wealth and broad domains
    Did not increase my care;
For hands were held to take the gains
    That I was glad to share.

XXXI.

My relatives were all unknown
    Since I was but a child,
When they had kind indulgence shown,
    And at my fancy smiled.

XXXII.

I gave them lands and all, except
　The home and treasures rare,
Some few of which I fondly kept
　My hermitage to share.

XXXIII.

The cabinet, and pictures all,
　Where tender memories dwell ;
But these, alas, would oft recall
　Thoughts that no tongue could tell.

XXXIV.

This is my story.　Let me pray
　That thou wilt now forgive
My seeming cruelty that day,—
　I have not long to live.

XXXV.

I've marked the character of her
　That charmed thy youthful heart.
Her beauty made my judgment err,—
　For wounds unhealed will smart.

61

XXXVI.

She had the same seductive grace
    That lured me, when a youth,
That memory I could not efface
    Nor trust in woman's truth.

XXXVII.

Her worth and true sincerity,
    Her modesty refined,
Her constant heart's fidelity
    Assure my doubting mind.

XXXVIII.

Come, Alvin! cheer my home and heart
    When Spring shall wake again.
Come! take my blessing and depart
    With love to soothe thy pain.

XXXIX.

To thee my childhood's home I give,
    With sylvan forests green,
For thee and thine,—I hope to live
    To see Eudora queen.

XL

Adieu! my child, my noble boy,
　　Haste quickly to my side,
That I may quaff a cup of joy
　　With thee and thy fair bride.

VII.

'Twas very hard my feelings to command;
I paused awhile to rest my weary hand;
Slower and fainter came each uttered word
Until the last was indistinctly heard.
Like ebbing tide when waters silently
Their tributes render to the grasping sea,
With fluctuating accents feebly came
In murmured syllables Eu-do-ra's name.✦
The nurse then entered, asked me to withdraw,
Saying, "The doctor's orders are my law."
At once I left, and met upon my way
Eudora, who inquired in manner gay,
"Where have you been?"

"Up to the hermitage,"
I answered, "writing for the learned Sage."
"What!—Do you mean you dared to write for him?
He chose you confidante? What an odd whim!
Words you may spin and weave in rhythmic tale,—
And yet you look quite serious and pale."

VIII.

"Look serious?—No, but glad as you will be
To know that poor man's mind at last is free
From unshared sorrow.

    He has told me all."
"Told you? How very strange! Did he recall
That morning by the brook?"

      Then suddenly
She paused with glance that fairly frightened me,
As if she had my meaning misapplied.
Laughing, I caught her hand, and softly sighed,
"Be not deceived, for I have just been taught
That good is sometimes out of evil brought.

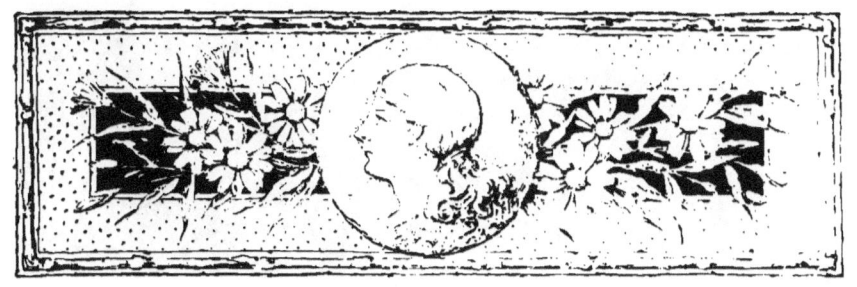

I wrote a letter in which every word
Flowed with the pensive sorrow that I heard."
"You wrote to—Alvin! Tell me all the rest!"
Eudora cried; and I could see her breast
Was heaving with excitement, as if she
Felt that her heart was struggling to be free.
"I wrote to Alvin; begged him to forgive
A cruel kinsman, who now prays to live
Until he blesses him and his first love.
'All's well that ends well.' Do you now approve?"

IX.

Bright blushes, flitting o'er her brow, enhanced
Her wondrous beauty as she stood entranced;
Then clasped me to her breast in long embrace,
Showering her tear-dewed kisses on my face.
"How I have loved," she said, "you only know;
My heart revives with happiness aglow.
Pray do not think me bold, unmaidenly,
If, in his praise, I speak adoringly,—
You darling dreamer!

Ever kind to me;
Your words have filled my cup with ecstasy.
To you alone such words I dare to speak;
The only consolation I could seek
Was silent musing on the hours passed
Down by the brook, where love bright visions cast."
She left me then, so near the close of day,
A flick'ring taper seemed the Sun's last ray
O'er crimson banners furling in the West,
Wooing the longest winter night to rest.

X.

That evening by the cheerful fire I told
The hermit's story; ill could I withhold
News that to all would bring such glad relief,
And mitigate an anxious mother's grief,—
The tender tribute to Eudora paid,
And generous promises to Alvin made,
Awoke compassion with the sufferer's pain
And prayers that he would soon his health regain.

CANTO IV.

I.

'Twas Christmas-tide, and brighter beamed our home:
My brothers for the holidays had come
With zest to join all games of pastime;—free
For any part in gladsome revelry.
The older, Ernest, was my father's joy,
His pride and hope.

           The younger, quite a boy,—
I called him Claude, but Claudius was his name,—
A devotee to Art, he toiled for fame.
The grave pursuit of letters for awhile
They had suspended, happy to beguile
The livelong day with seasonable mirth
And evening gatherings round the festive hearth.
Our hall was merry with its social cheer,
But out-door sports to boys are doubly dear.
I saw them building up a monstrous pile

Of snow-capped pillars in the Gothic style,
With fortresses to guard on either side
The gateway entrance, where high arches wide
Were formed of snow blocks; but too frail, alas!
For when beneath my father tried to pass,
Drawn by fleet horses in his dashing sleigh,
At once the massive pillars all gave way.

II.

Emerging from the avalanche of snow,
My father rose,—his face in ruby glow,—
Paternal dignity aside he laid,
And waging mimic warfare, soon repaid
The boys with snowballs like a gallant gay,
Until they both sought refuge from the fray.
Old Watch, our dog, as umpire, whimpering tried
To stay the game. The honors to divide,
He held dear father's coat in such a way
It was impossible for him to play.
I petted Watch, and coaxed him from his hold,
Which he released.—The conqueror then told

His vanquished foes that they the palm must yield,
And leave to him the honors of the field.
Then from his sleeves the crumbling snow he shook,
And laughingly the battle-field forsook.

III.

Next morning to our circle gayly came
Eudora with her mother—stately dame—
And aided us to deck a gorgeous tree,
When Claude, our artist, added jokingly,
"Eudora's pretty miniature must grace
The tip-top branch!   There I will proudly place
My first attempt to paint an angel fair,
With sunshine gleaming from her golden hair.
And light of love reposing in her eyes,
Blue as the depth of the celestial skies."
One figure there my memory can recall,
My brother Ernest, dignified and tall,
Watching the portrait by the artist's side,
As if the truthful likeness to decide.

71

Did he Eudora's tender glance mistake
Which thoughts of Alvin only could awake?

IV.

As touch on touch the artist's pencil gave,
The sunbeams lighted up each tress and wave,
Like saintly nimbus or pure vestal crown,
O'er her fair brow unsullied by a frown.
With joy we loved to watch creative power
That added life to beauty every hour.
Finished at last and on the tree-top placed,
Its throne of honor well the picture graced.
On the broad branches many tapers gleamed,
And twinkling lights like mimic meteors beamed;
The chandeliers their brilliant radiance shed,
As Ernest through the dance Eudora led,—
Through the time-honored, stately minuet,
As queen of beauty in that courtly set.
He gazed upon her with devoted pride,
As though no other could his glance divide;

And, as I watched awhile, a wish arose,
That friendship's voice forbade me to disclose.
I felt my heart with strange emotions swell,
To greet as sister one I loved so well,
Yet banished the disloyalty it bore,
And entertained the treacherous wish no more.

V.

Fairer than ever on that festive night
Her lithe form shone in robe of snowy white,
Of style antique, befitting queenly grace,
With flowing train draped with the finest lace;
No gem its lustre to her beauty lent,
With unadorned simplicity content.
My father danced with me in stately style,
Observing Ernest with a gracious smile:
Then whispered words intended for my ear,
" I fear your brother is in danger, dear!
'Twill never do.—You surely told him all,—
He must at once his wandering heart recall.
73

See you that smile?   The happy look he wears?
They rouse in me an anxious parent's cares
She loves another, Ernest ought to know,
'Tis thought of Alvin wakes the rosy glow,
That beams upon her face with fond delight.
Poor dazzled Ernest!   If he had the right
To claim Eudora as his lovely bride,
His choice would gratify our love and pride."

VI.

The music ceased,—the regal minuet,—
With parting courtesies closed the stately set.
The next cotillion's lively measures through,
With Ernest as my partner, fast we flew
To the inspiring music merrily,
His face alight with perfect ecstasy.
Soon as the figure gave a moment's rest,
Still nearer to my brother's side I pressed,
And whispered softly, " Alvin soon will come
To take Eudora to his distant home:
How we shall miss her."

74

"*Miss* is not the word,"

He answered, in a phrase I scarcely heard,
While gathered o'er his brow a sombre cloud,
As if the sunshine of his life to shroud;
And while we held our secret colloquy,
My father glanced at me approvingly.

VII.

Right gayly sped on fleeting wings the hours
That festive eve, among the holly bowers;
And from one chandelier there hung below
A garland formed of pearl-tipped mistletoe,
A mystical, uplifted Druid wreath
That merry maidens lightly skipped beneath;
For if at midnight hour a votress came,
Dreams would reveal her destined husband's name.
And at that moment gladsome chimes were borne
From pealing bells to herald Christmas morn.
With happy wishes blending each adieu,
Our friends from festive merriment withdrew.

75

I sought my couch, but no assuring dream,—
No sleep would come.   Confusing thoughts would teem
Through my poor head; forebodings that the love
Of Ernest for Eudora soon would prove
A fatal hindrance to his happiness ;
My only wish was that his love were less.
Slow passed the leaden hours till dawning day
Awoke with Orient hues in bright display,
Of glorious sunshine to illume the skies,
Tinting the snow-capt hills with warmer dyes,
Adding new pleasure to the joys of earth,
To celebrate our dear Redeemer's birth.

VIII.

The matin services divine were o'er,
And every face a smile of gladness wore.
On our return, there came a hasty scrawl,
Penned by the hermit, begging me to call
That Christmas morning, and be sure to bring
My friend Eudora, who, he hoped, would sing

One chant to cheer his loneliness and raise
His thoughts above the world in sacred praise,
And soothe his sufferings on that hallowed day.
To grant his wish, we hastened to obey.
My gentle friend had never been before
To see the Sage; and, as we passed the door,
He welcomed us with a most cordial smile.
Clasping our hands in silence for awhile,
He scanned Eudora's face as if to seek
Lost joys remembered that no words could speak;
The scene affected us with sad surprise,
When tears suffused his fondly glancing eyes.

IX.

Soon he with faltering voice exclaimed, "This bliss
Should win from thee, my child, a daughter's kiss."
Eudora, trembling, and with heaving breast,
Upon his brow her filial kisses pressed.
I left them thus,—no need had they of me,
There mingling tears in sacred sympathy.

Meeting the nurse, I said, persuasively,
" Pray, come with me into the library;
Let me look o'er the chants,—I will prepare
The simple part in which I am to share."
Thinking awhile in silence to remain,
I conned the music o'er and o'er again,
Until the nurse, impatient at delay,
Said, " Master will wonder if you longer stay."
I followed to the bedside, where still knelt
Eudora, listening to kind words.   I felt
Embarrassed till she, rising, took my hand,
Striving in vain her feelings to command;
Her warbled accents, musical and clear,
In trembling cadence fell upon the ear;
Then swelled in fuller tones sweet melody
Of Christmas anthems jubilant and free.

X.

My brothers soon were called from home away,
For college duties limited their stay;
Quite changed was Ernest,—haughty, cold, and sad,—

And we who knew the cause were very glad
To have him seek with zest his books once more,
With interest as great as e'er before;
Hoping hard study would relieve his woe.
Our artist, full of fun, though loath to go,
Left light of heart, his boyish fancy free
As any child's in love with art could be.
So passed the winter, with its pleasures gay,
The happy hours like dreams dissolved away;
Until the spring, its glories to acclaim,
With singing birds and vernal beauties came.
One morning with Eudora near the brook,
I suddenly exclaimed to her, " Do look,
There is the doctor beckoning to me!"
And, as I spoke, he joined us instantly,
Exclaiming, " Ah ! I find you both at last,"
As to Eudora he a letter passed.
The way he fumbled many papers o'er
Caused me to think the package others bore ;
My hand to him I held expectantly ;
Shaking his head, he answered teasingly,

" No letter for Miss Eila, but instead,
A verbal message ;—letters to be read
Await you now up at the hermitage.
The hermit cannot read each tear-stained page ;
He wishes you to visit him alone ;
Never before has he such interest shown.
Go you at once, your friend is entertained ;
Her sweet oblivion is far from feigned."
There sat Eudora, lost to all beside,
Her face aglow with warm exultant pride,
Drinking the wafted words from Alvin's pen
Breathing responsive love ; I left her then,
And hastened through the nearest path that led
Up the high bluff.   Beside the hermit's bed,
I read the letter, Alvin's fond reply,
Pausing, yet trying to suppress a sigh ;
Those words of gratitude were fond and free,
Yet there were threatening clouds of destiny.
It was not long before Eudora came,
Speaking with genial smile the hermit's name ;

She pressed a filial kiss upon his brow,
Saying, " I bring good news from Alvin now !
Yes, from dear Alvin, who may soon be here
Expectant hearts with happiness to cheer."

XII.

Observing then the letter in my hand,
She gayly said, " Ah ! now I understand
The reason why you left me all alone,
That you might share with our dear friend your own.
How kind and thoughtful.
                            What does Alvin say ?
May we expect him at an early day ?"
Confused were we, reluctant to destroy,
Until compelled, her momentary joy.
The hermit answered, " Welcome art thou here,
Thy charming presence every doubt shall cheer,—
The letter was to me.   Read it and find,
Although he'd gladly come, his duties bind."
Eudora read the letter slowly through,
Then, sighing, said, " Oh, it is sad and true,—

His joys, not sorrows, he would have me share ;
But gladly will I help him both to bear."

XIII.

Awhile we sat in silence, thinking o'er
The threatened dangers that the tidings bore.
Upon Eudora's face a new light spread,
Still sitting near the sufferer, she said,
" This is a shadow, Eila, such as you
Once traced in lines prophetically true ;
' We cannot have all sunshine,—needed night
Prepares us to enjoy the glorious light.' "
" 'Tis as I thought," the hermit gladly cried,
" Worthy art thou to be a hero's bride !—
And my amanuensis thou shalt be :
We will inspire him on to victory,
Quoting great Nelson's maxim all admire,   .
At duty's call to face the foeman's fire."
Eudora caught his hand impulsively,
Saying, " Your words I treasure fervently.

'Tis not less duty, but my joy to heed
His every wish."

           " Eila, once more, please read
The letter, for thou hast a stronger tone,
That every wish of his to us be known."
So spoke the hermit, and with accents clear
I read the letter held by all so dear.

To Mr. Alvin Alster,
      Burnel Bluffs,
           Westland.

I.

Dear parent of my new-born bliss,
   With joy my heart renewing,
In gratitude I write thee this,
   Thy words new hope induing.

II.

Ill can my pen due thanks express
   To thee in form of letter ;
So tame these words of happiness
   That gratitude doth fetter.

III.

Dear benefactor! Gracious sire!
  Thanks for thy generous measure;
The boon that meets my whole desire,
  This store of earthly pleasure.

IV.

Fain would I cast all care aside,
  However stern and binding,
To seek my love, my beauteous bride.
  And crown my joy in finding.

V.

Alas! this cruel destiny!
  My fate still unrelenting,
For lover's flight I am not free,
  Stern duty's call preventing.

VI.

My ship is ordered far away
  To distant wars now waging,
Where we must join in hostile fray,
  Our fleet the foe engaging.

VII.

To thee, dear sire, this news I send.
  The cause of my detention
Are perils that my way attend,
  Of which pray make no mention.

VIII.

Enclosed, for dear Eudora, find
  A note with love-lore teeming ;
Breathing no word to pain her mind,
  Or startle love's sweet dreaming.

IX.

To our friend Eila, stanch and tried,
  So tender, sympathetic,
Thou may'st my present care confide
  To her, with hope prophetic ;

X.

That she may hide in merry way,
  With pleasantry, concealing
From dear Eudora this delay,
  The danger not revealing.

My warmest thanks to her convey,
  And say, I hope to meet her
On my return most joyfully,
  With brother's love to greet her.

XII.

Oh, may it be not far away,
  When war shall cease dividing
My hopes, and bring our wedding day,
  With love and joy presiding.

Gratefully thine,
ALVIN.

CANTO V.

I.

THE glass of Time impeded seemed to be;—
So slowly moved the sands of destiny.
In daily visits to the hermitage
Eudora sought the counsel of the Sage.
She greeted him with blushes warm aglow,
Like rosebud melting with a touch the snow
Of frosty age. The hermit day by day
Improved in health, and often would repay
By kind instruction all we did for him.
With voice less tremulous, with eyes less dim,
Quoting wise apologues from classic lore,
The gathered gleanings from a boundless store,
Lessons for our instruction well designed,
New jewels from the thoughts of cultured mind,
With truths more potent than the tales of chance
That fascinate by folly's airy trance.

We heard his words by genius true inspired,
Bright like the diamond by rough usage fired,
With radiant lustre as Aladdin's gems,
More brilliant than those fabled diadems,—
They hold an honored seat in memory's hall,—
Would that my pen his thought-gems could recall.

II.

Early one morn we visited our friend
In kind communion one brief hour to spend;
With welcome greeting warm and genial smile
He strove by words of wisdom to beguile
Our thoughts from earth-born cares to heavenly themes,
Filling our minds with pure, poetic dreams.
" Behold," said he, " the heavens in grand display!
Their opening gates let forth the new-born day,
The infant morn encradled in bright gold,
While circling hours their rosy tints unfold.
Mark the uplifting veil of dewy mist!
See how the waking Sun hath warmly kissed
The glowing face of nature! Glorious sight!

90

" Behold," said he, the window come not

Beaming with radiant rays of dazzling light.
A crown of glory decks his sovereign head
And Orient splendors o'er his path are shed;
Pleased the Almighty's mandate to obey
'The greater light goes forth to rule the day.'"
He paused as if by some deep thought impressed,
Then turned, and pointing to the distant West,—
"Behold," said he, "the waning moon's cold beams!
How pales the argent in the golden gleams.
Slowly she passes, facing him the while,
And sinks below the steep with fainter smile,
By heavenly fiat rules the lesser light,
Imperial regent of the silent night.
Her car moves onward with majestic pace
Guided by laws divine: her placid face
From crescent gleaming 'neath the shade of earth
Grows till the harvest season kindles mirth.
The gleaners from their garners then repair
With joy in merry-making feast to share;
Thanking their bounteous Maker for the yield
Of much or little, from the cultured field.

Thrice happy they who joyfully receive
And in God's blessed providence believe.
Behold the flowers their grateful incense raise,
Dry their dew-tears and waft adoring praise
To Him who decked the lily of the vale
In modest white, like virgin pure and pale,
Who mantled Sharon's rose with blushes fair
And gave the violet royal robes to wear.
All blossoms blooming by his hand arrayed
To bask in sunshine or sequestered shade,
Each blade of grass, each leaf of shrub or tree
Mute thanks uplifts to God adoringly.

ADORATION

" Her homage to the Deity
All nature pays. Behold the sea !
In grandeur as they ebb and flow,
The waves to God are bowing low :
The waking flowers, the rising breeze,
The rustling leaves of plants and trees,

'Mid thousand charms that decked the Vessel

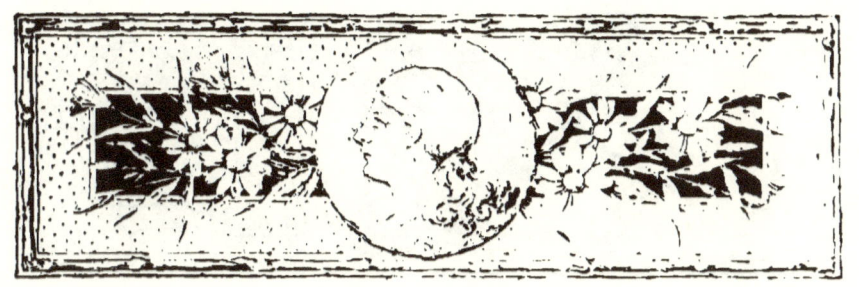

The birds with matin melody,
The patient kine on bended knee,
The insects floating in the air
With droning music,—everywhere,—
The notes of adoration swell
To Him who doeth all things well.
For God is love,—His works sublime
Declare his praise through endless time."

III.

He ceased, and o'er us, as a mantle fell
Unbroken silence like some mystic spell,
While we were seated in the open air
Our view extending over beauties rare.
'Mid thousand charms that decked the varied scene
The river rushing giant bluffs between,
Laving their base of hoary granite gray
Rolling impetuous on its outward way ;
With never-failing waters wild and free,
A ceaseless tribute to the sovereign sea.
Sacred our thoughts while silence thus ensued,
No lighter theme could on our minds intrude.

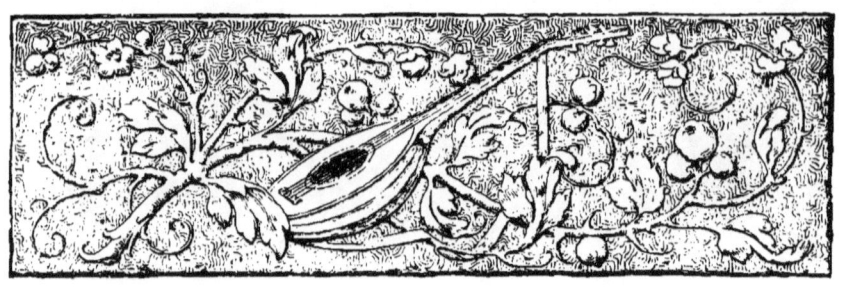

Do angels hover near and touch the cheek
Of one from silence first inspired to speak?
So was I taught, so trusted from a child,
At angel whispers slumbering infants smiled.
Eudora was the first, with praise sincere
She thanked our friend for leading her so near
The sacred portals of the heavens above,
Lifting her heart with adoration,—love
And faith, as flowers their fragrant incense raise,
And breathe sweet thanks that waft their Maker's praise,
" Thus all are blessed, by wisdom guided still,"
The hermit said, " obedient to God's will—

      " A shadow follows every one
        Whene'er he walks in sunny ways
        And meets the flood of brilliant rays,—
          A figure dun

     " Keeps pace with him ; or fast or slow,
        That ghostly shape is ever near,
        A dwarf or giant to appear
          In sombre show.

"On him whose life is free from guile,
  Who walks in paths of truth and light,
  All harmless falls the pall of night,
    Beneath God's smile.

"But whoso turns against the sun
  Beholds a dark form glide before
  With noiseless step his pathway o'er,
    The dusky one.

"In shadow he must ever tread
  Who chooses darkness for his way;
  On him the golden beams of day
    No radiance shed.

"May we as children of the light,
  Illumined by God's love divine,
  Still keep that path's unswerving line
    With sunbeams bright."

IV.

Three years had passed, with many changes rife
My brothers were at home, imparting life

To our sad circle.   Great anxiety
We felt for Alvin.   Rumors constantly
Were wafted to us; but from him no word,
Since his fond letter, had Eudora heard.
While thus our minds by hope and fear were tossed,
The tidings came that his good ship was lost.
From this we strove to guard Eudora's ears,
Yet knew she apprehended by her tears.
Pale grew her cheek with cold and silent grief;
No friend could soothe, no hope could bring relief;
Naught could alleviate her misery,
Until one morn she wildly came to me,
Seizing my hand, she cried, " What do they say?
What news from Alvin?
                                    Oh, this hapless day!
My heart is breaking now with tortures slow;
Despair succeeds to soul-consuming woe."
I could not, dared not, the sad tidings tell,
But kissed her pallid face I loved so well,—
" 'Tis idle gossip, nothing more," I said;
" You must have patience and by faith be led

Until detaining war shall end in peace,
And Alvin from his urgent charge release."

V.

Bright beamed Eudora's face; her smiles came back
Like sunshine breaking through a rifted rack;
Embracing me, she cried, " To you I owe
This new-born joy,—this hope's celestial glow,
From boding rumors cloaked in mystery.
How could they know?
                    There was no news for me:
Would I had earlier consulted you,
And felt those cruel tidings were not true:
You have illuminated life's dark page.—
Now let us visit our good friend, the Sage!
I have not been myself, my hope so dim,—
Therefore I had a dread of meeting him.
He looked on me so strangely sad and cold,
As if he strove some secret to withhold."
Though conscience whispered I had done amiss
Thus to impart a short-lived, groundless bliss,

Like ignis-fatuus to light her way,
With gayety my part I tried to play.
Entwining arms we visited our friend,
An hour in social cheer with him to spend;
His health improved, long walks he daily took.
Meeting there beside the babbling brook
He walked with us the winding path along.
I bade Eudora sing her favorite song;—

VI.

" Yes," said the hermit; " sing some melody
To rouse the sleeping echoes cheerily."
I saw he also had assumed a part
Of pleasantry to cheer Eudora's heart.
She, smiling, sang in silvery cadence clear
" The Brook,"—sweet madrigal we loved to hear:
And while I listened to the sparkling lay,
It seemed no longer time than yesterday
Since Alvin first into our presence came
And from Eudora took his scrap of game.

Then o'er my mind swift rushed the parting scene,
When, by the brook, the hermit came between
Her heart and its first fond awaking love,
Coldly her aspirations to reprove.
Since then more charming had Eudora grown,
Now, like a sylvan queen on vernal throne,
She sang as if inspired by memory,
Winning from me my fond idolatry.
My love had grown with admiration deep,
And in her presence ever would I keep
With true devotion, while her love for me
Was passive, loyal, and indulgently
She humored, like the whims of some pet child,
My varied moods and fancies ofttimes wild.

VII.

My brothers joined us now. " Be on the wing,"
I whispered Claude, " that contrast rare to bring:
Observe the austere hermit sitting there,
And see Eudora, like a vision fair."

Then Ernest, bending o'er me, sadly said,
" Another subject he may add instead."
" Whom do you mean?" I whispered, with surprise ;—
He answered not, save by suppressing sighs.
I felt annoyed, then listened to the song
That rippled with the rivulet along.
Soft fell the strains in cadence clear and low,
Waking the wavelets as the waters flow.
Until she ceased the sweet familiar strain,
And ended with the musical refrain,—

> " And out again I curve, I flow,
>   To join the brimming river ;
> For men may come and men may go,
>   But I go on forever——"

Then through the parting bushes I espied
Our long lost Alvin. " See ! oh, see !" I cried.
He only heard the last trilled word " forever"
From his Eudora's lips. " Yes, thine forever !"
He whispered, as he clasped her to his breast,
His happiness and fondest love expressed.

VIII

Then followed moments filled with silent joy.
The Sage exclaimed, "Thank God! my noble boy!
Thou hast returned to claim thy promised bride;—
I bless ye both with all a father's pride."
How tame are words describing scenes like this,—
The warm embrace, the tender welcome kiss,
The joyful greeting from all gathered there,
Save Ernest only,—he was then my care,—
To seek this brother, gladly would I go
Bid him take courage, aid him then to throw
Far, far away all thought of fated wrong,
And beg him join at once our happy throng.
Soon all had left.   Alvin beside his love
Passed through the path that led through maple grove
To Rosemont cottage, jubilant and gay.
'Twas the first visit that the Sage would pay,
With sympathetic joy, his face aglow,
As if exultant that the world should know
His new-found bliss.   Soon as they disappeared
I searched for Ernest, and what most I feared

Was realized.   Beneath an old gnarled oak,
Whose branches, rifted by the lightning stroke
And roughly twisted, formed a sheltered seat,
I found him hidden in that wild retreat.

IX.

Veiled by the mosses of its death-wrought shroud,
There sat my brother with his head low bowed
Upon his hands;—I saw his heaving breast,
His poor heart throbbing in its wild unrest.
"Ernest," I whispered, "this must never be;
Compose yourself to meet your destiny.
Eudora is so happy—Alvin true—
Congratulations from us all are due;
They have not missed you yet,—oh, come with me,
And let no other eyes this sadness see."
Around his neck my arms I gently twined,
With kisses fond and cheering words combined,
Striving to woo him from the hapless mood
That seared his heart, by jealousy imbued.

H. SIDDONS MOWBRAY

I coaxed, then scolded, and in my despair
I cried, " How can a man of spirit dare
Expose a misplaced love!   No one suspects,
But all will know what sullenness reflects."
Much more I said : he answered not the while,
Save by a frown and cold sardonic smile.
Old Watch was lying sadly at his feet ;
And when his worried look I chanced to meet.
With whining agony like human sighs.
He gazed upon me with sad speaking eyes.

X.

Then came a pause ; his answer I would wait
In silent prayer to stay his hapless fate ;
At last he cried, " You'd have me play a part
To hide the torture of a blighted heart ;
You argue well,—I go to join their glee ;
Her happiness shall not be marred by me.
For love like mine could never cause her pain.
Eila!   I thank you for this strength I gain."

As if awaking from a troubled dream
Of cruel fancies that would wildly teem
Through thoughts o'ercrowded with forebodings dark
His hope eclipsed yielded one radiant spark.
I twined my arms around his neck and pressed
My head upon his cold upheaving breast.
Responding to his words with glad surprise
I cried, " Dear Ernest, this is noble,—wise !"
Watch leaped upon us fawning with delight,
Then barking, bounding, through the path took flight.
Running as fleetly as if on a race,
Inducing us to join his mimic chase.
Great shaggy fellow, a good friend was he ;
Our joys and griefs he joined devotedly,
His countenance, alight when all was well,
Like mercury chilled, at any sadness fell.

XI.

The while we followed through the tangled way,
His buoyant happiness, his capers gay

Soon wooed our footsteps to his frolic speed
To join his play while following his lead,
Until we reached the happy throng, grown great
By friends and neighbors, to congratulate
Our dear Eudora's new-found happiness,
With pleasant words of love to greet and bless.
As pressing through the genial crowd we came,
Eudora, smiling, called " Ernest!" The name
Drew every glance toward us.   My face aglow
With joyous welcome, that they should not know
His agony of heart that clouds o'erspread,—
I stepping forward, took his place instead.
And then presented Ernest, who, meanwhile,
Received my badinage with placid smile ;
My father whispered, " I am happy now
To see your brother with unclouded brow."

XII.

Years passed away ; upon that mossy stone
Once more beside the stream I sat alone,—

"Come, Eila! We have waited long for you
Up at the Bluff. Come! tell us that tale, true,
The one you promised me that you would write.
Come! Do your best, dress it in sparkles bright."
So spake my brother Claude, and drove away
My plot of writing the superb display
Of that grand wedding ;—
                              Then the merry cheer
Of children laughing as they gathered near,
All hopping, skipping, romping in great glee,
Airing at once their messages for me,
From laughing, rosy lips, the bevy came
Wafting sweet kisses with endearing name;
Entreating me this story then to tell
On that same spot their mother loved so well.
They drew me from the past; for until then
My thoughts had wandered with my restless pen,
But Claude insisted. "At the Bluff they wait
To hear the incidents you will relate.
Come with me quickly to the hermitage
To cheer our friend, the noble, gifted Sage."

XIII.

"Yes," chimed the children. "Grandsire said you'd come
And tell us stories,—Please do tell us some!"
Chatting, they led the terraced path along,
Skipping with lightsome step to scraps of song,
Until we reached the bluff-crowned hermitage.
In his arm-chair the patriarchal Sage
Received with genial smiles our party gay.
The birds were trilling sweetly that bright day,
Through open windows wafting merrily
Their wooing notes, or calling cheerily.—
Alvin, the hero of this rhythmic tale,
Had grown in manly presence noble,—hale,—
Eudora happy,—genial,—dignified,
With matron grace that youthful charms outvied.
Her eldest daughter, like her mother, fair,
So like, with brother Ernest standing there,
Recalled to me that Christmas minuet
And those two stepping through the stately set.

XIV.

All looked so happy, so supremely glad;
The Sage with smiles said, "To thy story add
A sequel worthy of an honored place;
The threads of destiny we truly trace;
Content am I their fortunes to approve;
Happy are those who pledge their vows in love."
Surprised with joy that came so suddenly,
I glanced at Ernest, standing graciously
With his Eudora, loved, affianced bride,
Smiling on him with fondness by his side.
I hurried to them,—thanking God who gave
That lovely being to my brother brave;
Who now appeared in radiant happiness,
Gazing on one his every glance would bless.
Eudora clasped me in her dimpled arms
With blushes that enhanced her maiden charms,—
"Eila," said Ernest, "never until this
Could my affianced claim a sister's kiss."
Then Claude exclaimed, "Present your brother too,
To him who shares your joy, one kiss is due !"

Another subject for an artist's brush,—
I caught his arm, his sportive mood to hush.

XV.

Then spake the Sage, "Canst thou thy canvas stretch,
And make it large enough this group to sketch?
How many figures?" Claude, with mirthful smile,
Replied, "Yes—twenty,—in a little while
I'll have the present company all sketched;—
Be sure my canvas can be amply stretched.
A bachelor am I, who can recall
A dozen loves;—I could not wed them all.—
One subject I have painted, found her charms
In perfect figure, snowy rounded arms:
Another had dark, speaking hazel eyes
Within whose depths a hidden love-light lies:
And one, whose features formed in classic mould,
The purest lines of radiant beauty hold;
And one with golden crown of glorious hair,—"
I whispered Claude, "You've told enough, beware!"

He, laughing, answered, "Eila, I revere
Your warning, and the rest no one shall hear."
As gay at heart he left our presence,—then
The Sage exclaimed, "One of the best of men,
Devoted to his art, his works proclaim
A master's hand and promise future fame."

XVI.

Next morning Claude came to the hermitage;
In merry mood he offered to the Sage
A landscape, beautiful with sunny beams,
Lighting a rippling rill in golden gleams;
Beside the waters children were at play,
Bright as the sparkles of that glorious day.
Then said the Sage,—"Not twenty figures there."
"Yes," answered Claude, "but it has been my care
To let them wander through the woodland bowers;
We only see the children twining flowers."
My story let me close like Claude, "with care,"
And leave the children with their blossoms fair.

110